The Muppet Babies live in a nursery
in a house on a street that is a lot like yours.
But they can travel anywhere anytime using a special power—
the power of the imagination.
Can you imagine what it would be like to go with them?
Join the Muppet Babies on this adventure and find out.

Weekly Reader Presents

Baby Piggy
and the Thunderstorm

By Joanne Barkan • Illustrated by Tom Cooke

Muppet Press
New York

This book is a presentation of
Weekly Reader Books.

Weekly Reader Books offers book clubs for children
from preschool through high school.

For further information write to:
Weekly Reader Books
4343 Equity Drive
Columbus, Ohio 43228

Printed in the United States of America.

DAZZLE, ZAP! CRASH, BOOM!
 Outside the Muppet Baby nursery, lightning flashed, and thunder rolled through the sky. The clouds were as dense and dark as ink. The rain came down hard and fast, pounding against the window.

"It sure is raining cats and dogs," said Kermit.

"Cats and dogs!" Baby Piggy disagreed. "It's not raining cats and dogs. It's raining rain—buckets and tubs and oceans full of rain."

Piggy shivered and snuggled deeper into her armchair. She didn't like thunderstorms at all.

"It might rain so long that it rains right into the nursery," worried Piggy.

"That won't happen," answered Kermit. "It's just a summer storm. They never last too long."

But Piggy put up her pink striped umbrella—just in case.

"This storm is too scary for me," Piggy shivered.

"Don't worry," said Kermit. "You're safe as long as you're inside."

But Piggy put on her raincoat and rainhat and hid behind the chair—just in case.

Kermit tried again to help. "Nanny told me all about thunderstorms," he explained. "Lightning is electricity. It heats up the air, and that makes thunder."

"I'm still worried," insisted Piggy.

Then she gathered up her two favorite dresses, a warm sweater, some raisin cookies left over from lunch and packed them in her waterproof suitcase—just in case.

"Try to be patient," suggested Kermit. "You just have to wait for some things to end."

Piggy nodded. She heard Kermit, but she went on wiggling herself as far as she could underneath the bed—just in case.

A moment later, a long streak of lightning pierced the sky, and a great thunderclap shook the nursery. Piggy squeezed her eyes shut.

When she opened her eyes, Piggy was looking up at a large dog holding a baton.

"Welcome to World Storm Headquarters," said the dog. "I'm the Great Rain Dane. Right here behind me are the Thunderclap Cats and the Lightning Pups."

"Thunderclap Cats and Lightning Pups?" thought Piggy. "They must be the ones who are making it rain cats and dogs."

Before she could utter a word, the Great Rain Dane spoke again. "You'll have to excuse us," he said politely. "We're in the middle of a storm right now. Why don't you sit down and enjoy the show?"

The Rain Dane signaled to the Cats and Pups with his baton. DAZZLE, ZAP! The Lightning Pups bounced their beams across the sky. CRASH, BOOM! The Thunderclap Cats used their cymbals to make the thunder roll. And when the Great Rain Dane tapped his foot, the rain came down even faster.

As Piggy took her seat, the Lightning Pups were beginning a short solo. Piggy was feeling a little hungry as well as worried, so she ate her leftover raisin cookies and then glanced around for a refreshment stand. But there was nothing in sight.

"Oh, dear," Piggy sighed as she watched the band play. "They're really having fun. They'll probably play for a long, long time. They'll probably play so long that…

…everything in the nursery will get damp and soggy, especially the food in the kitchen. Then there will be no crispy toast and crunchy cereal for breakfast."

"It will probably rain so long that when lunchtime comes around, there will be no more picnic lunches. All the picnic blankets will have floated out to sea, and that means all the peanut butter sandwiches and cupcakes will have floated away, too."

"Dinner will be very, very late because Nanny will have to swim while she prepares it. Oh, no! Does Nanny know how to swim?"

"When it's time to go to bed, we'll probably have to sleep on rubber rafts and wear waterproof pajamas. And how will we be able to eat our bedtime snack?"

Piggy was getting more worried and hungry every minute. "Mr. Great Rain Dane," she shouted above the noise of the thunder and rain. "When is this storm going to end?"

The Rain Dane continued waving his baton and tapping his foot as he turned to speak to Piggy. "Try to be patient," he called out. "You just have to wait for some things to end."

"That sounds familiar," said Piggy.

The Thunderclap Cats stepped up to the front of the stage to do their solo.

"Hm-m…" wondered Piggy, "won't all this rain make their cymbals get rusty and break?"

"What if all the cymbals in the whole world get rusty and break? And what about all the xylophones and trumpets and flutes and kazoos?"

This reminded Piggy that Nanny had promised to
take the Babies to a concert in the park that night.
"But if all the instruments get rusty and break, there
won't be any concert, and that means no ice cream at
intermission."

"If there are no instruments left in the world, there will be no music for the circus. Then there will be no circus, and that means no hot dogs or cotton candy. There will be no music for the movies, no movies, and that means no popcorn."

"And then there won't even be music for the skating rink, no skating rink, and that means…that means…NO HOT CHOCOLATE WITH MARSHMALLOWS!"

Piggy jumped up. "Mr. Great Rain Dane, stop right now! If you keep playing, everything will get wet and rusty. There will be no music, no fun things to do, and nothing to eat!"

The Great Rain Dane shook his head. "Don't worry. That won't happen. The Cats and Pups and I love to play up a storm, but we know when to end the show. Listen."

The Great Rain Dane was right. The boom of the cymbals was growing faint. The flashing lights dimmed. The pounding rain became a light patter and then stopped. One by one, the Cats and Pups sat down to rest. It was very quiet.

"You see," whispered the Great Rain Dane, "you just have to wait—"

"I know—you just have to wait for some things to end," repeated Piggy as she opened her eyes.

Baby Kermit was pointing to the nursery window. "Look. The sun's out," he said. "Now would you like me to finish explaining what makes thunderstorms happen?"

"Oh, I would just love to hear all about it," replied Piggy sweetly, "but some other time. Right now, let's go outside and play."

The storm had left a large puddle in the middle of the garden. Piggy and Kermit decided to go sailing.

As she leaned back in her deck chair and sipped a big glass of lemonade, Piggy smiled. Thunderstorms weren't so bad after all—as long as you stayed dry.